Barbie
i can be...

A Pastry Chef

Concept developed for Mattel by Egmont Creative Center
By Freya Woods
Illustrated by TJ Teams

Random House 🏠 New York

Published in the United States by Random House Children's Books, a division of Random House, Inc.,
1745 Broadway, New York, NY 10019, and in Canada by Random House of Canada Limited, Toronto.
No part of this book may be reproduced or copied in any form without permission from the copyright owner.
Random House and the colophon are registered trademarks of Random House, Inc.
ISBN: 978-0-307-93114-6
randomhouse.com/kids   MANUFACTURED IN CHINA   10 9 8 7 6 5 4 3 2 1

Barbie and Teresa are very excited—they are going to spend the day working at Teresa's family's bakery.

"I've always dreamed of being a pastry chef," Barbie says.

"Don't forget to come to my house at five o'clock for the party!" says Nikki.

"We wouldn't miss it!" Barbie and Teresa say together.

"I'm so glad you're here," Teresa's mom says to Barbie and Teresa. "Could you do the baking while I work at the counter? We're extra busy today."

"We'll get started right away," Teresa says as she hands Barbie a pastry chef's jacket.

Barbie and Teresa quickly get to work. Soon they have baked some delicious-looking chocolate chip cookies!

"I've got to deliver these cookies," says Teresa. "Do you think you can bake a chocolate cherry cake on your own?"

"Sure," Barbie says, beginning to sift the flour. "Leave it to me!"

Barbie mixes all the ingredients together, then places the cake pan in the oven. A short while later, she ices and decorates her beautiful chocolate cherry cake. But when Barbie is carrying the cake to the refrigerator, Teresa swings the kitchen door open and knocks it right out of her hands. *Splat!*

"Oh, no!" cries Teresa.

"We'd better bake another cake right away," says Barbie.

"I'll clean up this mess," says Teresa.

"I'll go to the store to get more chocolate and cherries," says Barbie.

Barbie changes out of her chef's jacket and hurries outside. The streets are suddenly crowded.

"Where did all these people come from?" Barbie asks as she buys some chocolate at the candy store.

"There's a parade today," the woman behind the counter explains.

As Barbie walks to the fruit market, a policeman stops her. "The road to the market is closed today because of the parade," he explains. "You'll have to go through the park."

Barbie is worried. If she walks all the way through the park, she won't have time to get back to the shop and bake the cake before Nikki's party.

Suddenly, Barbie spots Ken. She waves at him through the crowd.

"Hi, Ken!" says Barbie. "Can I borrow your skateboard?"

Barbie whizzes through the park on Ken's skateboard. She gets to the market quickly and buys some cherries. Then she races back to the bakery.

"Let's get baking!" Barbie says as she bursts through the kitchen door.

Barbie and Teresa quickly mix all the ingredients and put the cake in the oven. Then Teresa puts the finishing touches on some cookies.

Barbie carefully arranges the chocolate and cherries on top of the cake. "I think this one is even better than the one I dropped!" she says, laughing. "Thanks for showing me how to be a pastry chef, Nikki."

Teresa's mom is very impressed by Barbie and Teresa's work. "Everything looks amazing!" she exclaims.

At Teresa's house, Barbie and Teresa change for the party. When they are ready to leave, Teresa's mother hands them two big cake boxes. "You deserve a treat after all your hard work!" she says.

At the party, everyone wants to know about Barbie and Teresa's day at the bakery.

"It was so much fun," Barbie tells them. "And best of all, we've brought dessert!"

"What a wonderful cake!" exclaims Nikki. "You should be a pastry chef!"

"Working in the bakery was harder than I thought it would be, but Teresa taught me so much," says Barbie. "Maybe I *can* be a pastry chef!"

© Mattel

"Thanks for saving me," says Raquelle.

"I'm so glad I could help you," replies Barbie. "All the training was worth it, and now I know I *can* be a lifeguard!"

Woof! Woof! Sadie agrees.

"Well done, Barbie!" says Justin. "You're a great lifeguard."

"Thanks!" replies Barbie as she puts a towel around Raquelle's shoulders.

"Now hang on tight and I'll pull you to shore," says Barbie.
Raquelle wraps her arms around the life buoy as Barbie
carefully swims through the rough waters.

The crowd on the beach cheers when they see that
Raquelle has been saved.

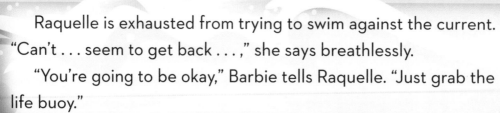

Raquelle is exhausted from trying to swim against the current. "Can't . . . seem to get back . . . ," she says breathlessly.

"You're going to be okay," Barbie tells Raquelle. "Just grab the life buoy."

"Summer, blow your whistle to alert the other lifeguards!" cries Barbie.

She dives into the ocean and swims as fast as she can toward Raquelle.

Soon the beach gets very crowded. Barbie and Summer watch all the swimmers carefully.

"Look over there!" exclaims Barbie. "Someone is out in the no-swimming area."

"It's Raquelle!" Summer cries as she looks through her binoculars. Barbie leaps down from the lifeguard tower to help her friend.

"Hi," says Raquelle. "We're going to see who can swim the farthest."

"Be careful," warns Barbie. "The bay may look calm, but it can be really dangerous."

"I'm a good swimmer," says Raquelle. "See you later!"

After practice, Barbie notices Raquelle and Teresa jogging along the beach.

Barbie and Justin team up for rescue practice. They swim
out, then take turns pulling each other back in.

Later, Summer and Barbie watch as the lifeguards practice rescuing each other. One lifeguard goes out in the water and floats motionless. The other lifeguard pulls him back to shore. "I'm up next," says Barbie.

"Labradors like Sadie make great lifeguards," explains Justin. "They love swimming and are natural retrievers. They'll fetch anything, from a Frisbee to a swimmer in trouble."

Woof! Woof!

"Here comes the best lifeguard on our whole team!" says Justin. "Isn't that right, Sadie?"

"She's adorable!" exclaims Barbie.

"Summer and I will put green flags out in the area of the bay where it's safe to swim," says Justin, the head lifeguard.

Barbie and her friend Summer have just completed their lifeguard training, and it's their first day working at the beach.

"Looks like high winds and rough seas today," Barbie says. "I'd better put the red flags up to warn the swimmers."

A Lifeguard

Concept developed for Mattel by Egmont Creative Center
By Susan Marenco, based on plots written by Giulia Conti
Illustrated by Tino Santanach and Joaquin Canizares

Random House 🏠 New York

BARBIE and associated trademarks and trade dress are owned by, and used under license from, Mattel, Inc.
Copyright © 2012 Mattel, Inc. All Rights Reserved.
Published in the United States by Random House Children's Books, a division of Random House, Inc.,
1745 Broadway, New York, NY 10019, and in Canada by Random House of Canada Limited, Toronto.
No part of this book may be reproduced or copied in any form without permission from the copyright owner.
Random House and the colophon are registered trademarks of Random House, Inc.
ISBN: 978-0-307-93114-6
randomhouse.com/kids   MANUFACTURED IN CHINA   10 9 8 7 6 5 4 3 2 1